**W9-ASD-233**

Leonard

WOLF ERLBRUCH

ORCHARD BOOKS   NEW YORK

Leonard loved dogs. He knew everything about them. He knew every breed and which ones had pointed or floppy ears.

When Leonard said, "That's not a Dalmatian," it clearly wasn't.

Most importantly, Leonard knew that dogs had big, sharp teeth. And *that* was the problem.

E

very morning Leonard woke his mother and father with a few barks and yelps. "Our little doggie is awake," groaned his father.

L

eonard barked out the window every morning.
The neighbors were not pleased.

Leonard often visited his grandmother. She was seventy-nine years old and lived upstairs. She was always happy when her favorite grandson stopped in. But sometimes she wished he would play a regular game with her like hide-and-seek or go fish.

L

eonard loved to go shopping with his mother, but sometimes he got into trouble.

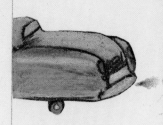

T

hough Leonard loved dogs, whenever he passed one on the street, even a puppy, he was terrified.

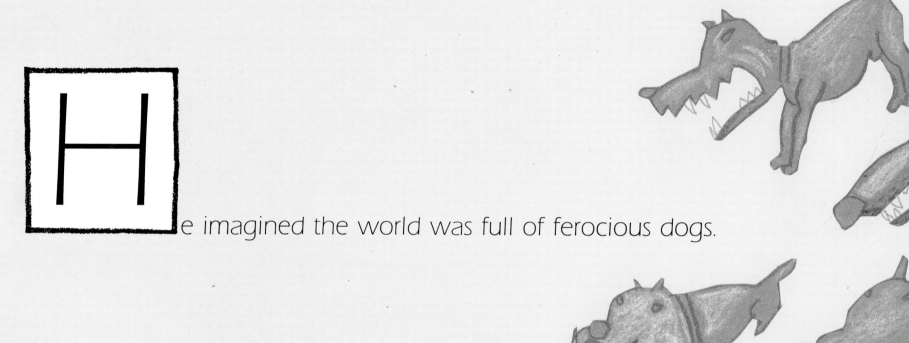

H
e imagined the world was full of ferocious dogs.

One night he couldn't fall asleep. All he could think of were dogs and teeth. Suddenly a tiny fairy fluttered down onto his bedspread. Leonard was surprised. He had always imagined fairies to be at least as big as his friend Brenda. In her fairy voice she told him, "You may make one wish."

Leonard didn't hesitate. "I'd like to be a big, strong dog!"

"What kind?"

"Spotted, please."

The next morning Leonard woke his parents as usual. "Our little doggie is awake," his father said sleepily.

His mother and father were both surprised when Leonard leapt onto the bed.

They cried and cried but felt better when they realized what a good dog he was.

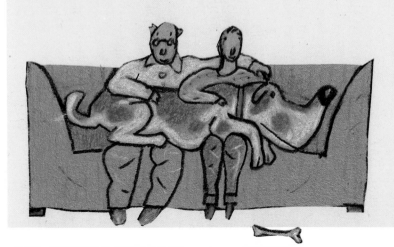

They built him his very own house in the backyard and only cried a little when telling their story.

Leonard was the happiest dog in the world until he took his first walk. Then something unexpected happened.

He imagined the world was full of ferocious little boys.

That night Leonard bellowed sadly at the moon.

"Your wish didn't turn out so well," chirped a familiar voice. "But since you're so sad, I'll let you make one more."

Leonard whispered in her ear.

"Are you sure?" she asked.

He nodded his heavy head.

T he next morning was quiet. Leonard slipped into his parents' bed. When they woke up, they were overwhelmed with joy. Their little boy was back! They hugged and kissed him so hard and for so long that Leonard began to growl—just a little.

For Leonard

Orchard Books, 95 Madison Avenue, New York, NY 10016

Manufactured in the United States of America
Printed by Barton Press, Inc.
Bound by Horowitz/Rae
Book design by Jean Krulis
The text of this book is set in 20 point Eras Light.

10 9 8 7 6 5 4 3 2 1

Library of Congress Cataloging-in-Publication Data
Erlbruch, Wolf.
[Leonard. English]
Leonard / by Wolf Erlbruch. — 1st American ed.
p.   cm.
Summary: Leonard, who loves dogs but is rather afraid of them, asks a fairy
to turn him into a dog so that he can undergo the canine experience himself.
ISBN 0-531-09482-0 — ISBN 0-531-08782-4 (lib. bdg.)
[1. Dogs—Fiction. 2. Fear—Fiction. 3. Fairies—Fiction.] I. Title.
PZ7.E72594Le   1995   [E]—dc20   95-10294